W9-CDO-192

R00954 14545

# JULIUS LESTER

# THE KNEE-HIGH MAN
## and Other Tales

THE CHICAGO PUBLIC LIBRARY

ORIOLE PARK BRANCH
5201 N. OKETO AVENUE
CHICAGO, ILLINOIS
60656

*pictures by*

# RALPH PINTO

*A Puffin Pied Piper*

ORIOLE PARK BRANCH
7454 W. BALMORAL AVE.
CHICAGO, IL 60656

DISCARD

To Jody and Malcolm,
who never fall asleep when
I tell them these stories

Dial Books for Young Readers
A Division of Penguin Books USA Inc.
375 Hudson Street
New York, New York 10014

Text copyright © 1972 by Julius Lester
Pictures copyright © 1972 by Ralph Pinto
All rights reserved
Library of Congress Catalog Card Number: 72-181785
Printed in Hong Kong by South China Printing Co.
First Pied Piper Printing 1985
COBE
10  9  8  7

A Pied Piper Book is a registered trademark of
Dial Books for Young Readers,
a division of Penguin Books USA Inc.
® TM 1,163,686 and ® TM 1,054,312

THE KNEE-HIGH MAN *and Other Tales*
is published in a hardcover edition by
Dial Books for Young Readers.
ISBN 0-14-054810-6

R00954 14545

# Contents

What Is Trouble?  5

Why Dogs Hate Cats  9

Mr. Rabbit and Mr. Bear  12

Why the Waves Have Whitecaps  21

The Farmer and the Snake  24

The Knee-High Man  27

A Note About the Stories  30

ORIOLE PARK BRANCH
7454 W. BALMORAL AVE.
CHICAGO, IL. 60656

# What Is Trouble?

One day Mr. Rabbit was walking down the road when he met Mr. Bear.

"How're you today, Mr. Rabbit?" Mr. Bear said.

"I got trouble, Mr. Bear," Mr. Rabbit replied, shaking his head.

"Trouble?"

"I got so much trouble, I don't know what I'm going to do. I've got trouble with my children and trouble with my house and just all kinds of trouble, Mr. Bear. What am I going to do?"

Mr. Bear looked puzzled. "What do you mean, Mr. Rabbit?"

"What do you mean what do I mean? I just told you. I got trouble."

"I heard what you said, Mr. Rabbit. But just what is trouble?"

"What?" Mr. Rabbit exclaimed, leaping up in the air. "You don't know what trouble is? Haven't you ever had trouble?"

The bear shook his head. "I don't think so. If I did have trouble, I didn't know anything about it."

"Where've you been, Mr. Bear, that you've never had trouble?"

"Well, I sleep all through the winter. The rest of the time I'm in the woods collecting food for my family. You know, we have to eat a lot so that we can sleep through the cold winter when we can't find much food."

The rabbit smiled. "Mr. Bear, I'm going to do you a favor."

"What's that?"

"I'm going to show you what trouble is."

"Oh, would you, Mr. Rabbit?" the bear said happily. "That's mighty nice of you."

"Mr. Bear, it's my pleasure, believe me." They were walking across a grassy meadow and Mr. Rabbit said, "I want you to lie down right here and go to sleep, Mr. Bear. When you wake up, you'll know what trouble is."

So Mr. Bear lay down and was soon asleep. The minute he was, Mr. Rabbit set the meadow on fire. As soon as Mr. Bear smelled the smoke, he woke up. He leaped to his feet, and all around him the grass was on fire. He ran from one side to the other yelling, "Trouble! Trouble!" Finally he saw one small place that hadn't begun to burn yet, and he leaped through to safety, yelling, "Trouble! Trouble!"

A short distance away Mr. Rabbit sat under a tree laughing so hard he was crying. "Now you know, Mr. Bear!" he yelled.

"I know," Mr. Bear yelled back, "but if I ever catch you, Mr. Rabbit, you'll have more trouble than you've ever had in your life."

But by that time Mr. Rabbit had hopped into the forest and out of sight, laughing as he went.

# Why Dogs Hate Cats

Once upon a time the dog and the cat used to be the best of friends. There weren't any two animals anywhere who were better friends. They worked, played, and even ate together. But they liked to eat together more than anything else in the world.

Their favorite food was ham. Every chance they had, they'd buy a piece of ham. One day both of them had some extra money saved and the dog said to the cat, "We have some extra money, Mr. Cat, but neither you nor I has enough to get a whole ham by himself. Now, if we put your money and my money together, we'll have enough money to get that ham."

So they went to town and bought a ham. It was a big ham, and it was so big and so heavy that they had to take turns carrying it. The dog carried it first and as he walked down the road, he sang, "Our ham! Our ham! Our ham!"

When it was the cat's turn to carry it, he sang, "My ham! My ham! My ham!" The dog heard what the cat was singing, but he didn't say anything.

When it came the dog's turn again, he sang, "Our ham! Our ham! Our ham!"

But when the cat carried the ham the next time, he sang, "My ham! My ham! My ham!"

The dog said, "Tell me, Mr. Cat, why do you sing, 'My ham?' It is our ham, isn't it?"

The cat didn't say a word, but kept on singing, "My ham! My ham! My ham!" And the dog continued to sing, "Our ham! Our ham! Our ham!"

When they were almost home, the cat was carrying the ham when all of a sudden he ran up a tree and sat down on a limb and ate the whole ham by himself. The dog was angry, and he barked and jumped and growled and snarled. But he couldn't climb a tree, so there was nothing he could do. But he told the cat, "I can't get you now, Mr. Cat, but when you come down out of that tree, I'm going to chase you until you drop."

And that's the reason that every time a dog sees a cat, he'll chase it. The dog is still mad at the cat for eating up all the ham.

# Mr. Rabbit and Mr. Bear

If there was one thing in the world Mr. Rabbit liked, it was lettuce. He would do anything to get lettuce. Well, one day Mr. Rabbit was hopping down the road, and he noticed suddenly that he was passing a field of lettuce. Mr. Rabbit had never seen so much lettuce in all his life. As far as he could see, there were rows and rows and rows and rows of lettuce. And the only thing that stood between Mr. Rabbit and those rows and rows and rows and rows of lettuce was a wire fence.

Mr. Rabbit hopped alongside the fence for a minute trying to decide the best way to get to the lettuce. He looked up at the fence and knew that it was too high for him to jump over. He looked down at the ground and for a moment thought about digging a hole and crawling under. But that was too much work. He took a good look at the holes in the wire, but they were too small for him to squeeze through.

"What am I going to do?" said Mr. Rabbit. "I have to have some of that lettuce."

Anybody else would have given up, but not Mr. Rabbit. He went across the road and sat down under a big oak tree

12

to think the situation over. He hadn't been sitting there long before a little girl walked across the road, opened the gate to the field of lettuce, and went inside.

"That's it!" Mr. Rabbit shouted, leaping up. "Tomorrow I'll come here at the same time, and if the little girl comes again, I'll get her to let me in."

The next day Mr. Rabbit was sitting by the gate waiting for the little girl. After a while she came out of the woods.

"Good morning, little girl," said the rabbit, hopping over to her.

"Good morning, Mr. Rabbit."

"The farmer told me to ask you to let me into the field."

"Oh, certainly, Mr. Rabbit," the little girl said. She opened the gate and Mr. Rabbit hopped through.

"Thank you," said Mr. Rabbit. "Now you be sure and come let me out at noon."

"All right, Mr. Rabbit."

Well, Mr. Rabbit hopped to a far corner of the field and began eating. He had never tasted such delicious, scrumptious, crispy, luscious, delectable, exquisite, ambrosial, nectareous, yummy lettuce in aaaaaaall of his life. And he ate and ate and ate and then ate some more. When noon came, he was ready to go. He'd eaten so much that it was all he could do to hop to the fence and have the little girl let him out.

But the next day he was sitting outside the gate, ready for another morning of that delicious, scrumptious, crispy, luscious, delectable, exquisite, ambrosial, nectareous, yummy lettuce. Every morning Mr. Rabbit came back and every morning the little girl let him in.

After several weeks the farmer started noticing that a lot of his lettuce was missing. He asked everyone he knew if they knew anything about it, but no one did. So he decided to hide behind a tree and see if he could learn who had been eating his lettuce.

The next morning he was there bright and early, and he saw Mr. Rabbit hop up to the gate. Then he saw his little girl come out of the woods, cross the road, and open the gate to let Mr. Rabbit into his field of delicious, scrumptious, crispy, luscious, delectable, exquisite, ambrosial, nectareous, yummy lettuce. The farmer was angry, but not at his little girl. He knew that Mr. Rabbit had tricked her, and he was sure angry at the rabbit.

He waited until he was certain that Mr. Rabbit was busy eating lettuce. Then he sneaked into the field.

Mr. Rabbit didn't know that his lettuce-eating days were almost over. He was too busy enjoying that lettuce. Chomp! Chomp! Chomp! He was eating so fast that he didn't hear the farmer. The first thing he knew someone was holding him by the scruff of his neck, yelling, "I got you, Mr. Rabbit! I got you!" The farmer laughed. "You were trying to eat up all of my lettuce. But I got you now! I'm going to teach you a lesson, Mr. Rabbit."

The farmer took Mr. Rabbit out to a big tree. There he tied a rope around one of his legs and tied the other end of the rope to a limb of the tree. And there was poor Mr. Rabbit, hanging in the middle of the air by one leg, swinging back and forth.

16

"I'm going to leave you there for a while, Mr. Rabbit. That'll teach you a lesson."

The farmer went away, leaving Mr. Rabbit swinging back and forth, back and forth. Anybody else would've been scared hanging up there in the middle of the air by one leg. But not Mr. Rabbit. He was already busy thinking about how he was going to get down.

He was thinking and thinking and thinking, swinging back and forth, back and forth. He was thinking so hard that he didn't notice Mr. Bear walking down the road.

Mr. Bear looked up and saw Mr. Rabbit swinging back and forth, back and forth. "Uh . . . Mr. Rabbit?"

Mr. Rabbit was thinking so hard he didn't hear him.

"Mr. Rabbit!" the bear shouted.

"Oh! Hello, Mr. Bear. How're you this morning?" the rabbit said.

"Fine. Fine. How're you, Mr. Rabbit?"

"Oh, just fine. Just fine. I'm taking it easy."

"Mr. Rabbit?"

"What is it, Mr. Bear?"

"Uh . . . could you tell me what you're doing up there?"

"Can't you tell, Mr. Bear?" Mr. Rabbit said. "I'm resting."

"Resting?"

"Yep."

Mr. Bear scratched his head. "Looks to me like you're tied to that limb by one leg."

"That's right, Mr. Bear. And that's the new way of resting."

"It is?" asked Mr. Bear.

"Yes, it is," said Mr. Rabbit. "It's much better than lying down in a bed."

"You wouldn't mind if I tried it, would you, Mr. Rabbit?"

Mr. Rabbit thought for a minute. "Well, I don't know, Mr. Bear."

"Aw, please, Mr. Rabbit."

"Well, all right. But you have to promise not to rest too long, Mr. Bear. I know you. You'll get up here and enjoy it so much that I'll never get to rest again."

"I promise, Mr. Rabbit. I just want to try it for a minute."

"O.K. Take this rope off my leg."

Mr. Bear reached up and took the rope off Mr. Rabbit's leg. Mr. Rabbit jumped down to the ground. Then he helped Mr. Bear put his leg through the rope and pulled the loop tight. "There you are, Mr. Bear. Doesn't that feel good?"

Mr. Bear was swinging back and forth, upside down, but he nodded. "It sure does, Mr. Rabbit."

"Well, I'm going down to the creek to get me a drink of water, Mr. Bear. I'll be back in a few minutes."

"O.K., Mr. Rabbit."

But Mr. Bear never saw Mr. Rabbit again that day. Late that evening when the farmer came back to see if Mr. Rabbit had learned his lesson, he was surprised and angry when he saw Mr. Bear hanging up there instead. But Mr. Rabbit was long gone by that time. All the farmer could do was let Mr. Bear down and hope that he would catch Mr. Rabbit another time.

# Why the Waves Have Whitecaps

Long, long ago the wind and the water were the closest of friends. Every day Mrs. Wind would visit Mrs. Water, and they would spend the day talking. Mostly they enjoyed talking about their children. Especially Mrs. Wind. "Just look at my children," Mrs. Wind would say. "I have big children and little children. They can go anywhere in the world. They can stroke the grass softly, and they can knock down a tree. They can go fast or they can go slowly. Nobody has children like mine."

Every day Mrs. Wind would talk this way about her children. After a while Mrs. Water began to get very angry with Mrs. Wind for the way she always bragged about her children.

One day Mrs. Wind's children came to her. "Mother, we're thirsty. Can we get a cool drink of water?"

"Just run over to Mrs. Water and hurry right back," she told them.

The children went over to Mrs. Water. But when they got there, Mrs. Water grabbed them. "I'll teach Mrs. Wind to

brag about her children all the time." And she drowned all of
Mrs. Wind's children.

When her children did not come back, Mrs. Wind began to
worry. She went down and asked Mrs. Water if she had seen
them. "No," said Mrs. Water.

But Mrs. Wind knew her children had gone there, so she
blew herself over the ocean, calling her children. Every time

she called, little white feathers appeared on top of the water. And that's why there are whitecaps on the waves to this very day. They're Mrs. Wind's children trying to answer her. Whenever there is a storm on the water, it's Mrs. Wind and Mrs. Water fighting over the children. And the whitecaps on the waves are the children trying to tell their mother where they are.

# The Farmer and the Snake

One cold winter morning a farmer was walking down the road. He hadn't gone far when he noticed a snake lying in the road. He stopped and looked at the snake. It was so cold that it couldn't move. The farmer was a very kind-hearted man, and he felt sorry for the snake. So he bent over and picked it up. It was frozen so solid that it was as stiff and hard as a log. The farmer put the snake inside his coat where it could get warm and thaw out. The farmer felt good about his kind act, and after a while he began to feel something moving around inside his coat. He peeked in. "Hello there, Mr. Snake. Are you getting warmed up?"

The snake didn't say anything.

Sometime later the snake wriggled harder. The farmer took another look at him. "You seem to be almost thawed out now."

"Almost," the snake said, flicking his forked tongue.

"Well, Mr. Snake, I sure am happy. You would've frozen to death if I hadn't picked you up. Now I want you to promise me that you won't bite me when you get all

thawed out. Remember, I did you a big favor."

The snake nodded. "I appreciate it, Mr. Farmer. I really do. And you don't have to worry. I won't bite you."

"That's good."

Just as the farmer got close to town, the snake started moving around, and the farmer knew that he was all thawed out. The farmer opened up his coat, and the snake crawled out and bit the farmer on the neck.

"Mr. Snake!" the farmer cried. "You promised that you wouldn't bite me."

The snake looked at the farmer and said, "That's what I promised, Mr. Farmer, but I'm a snake. You knew that when you picked me up. And you knew that snakes bite. It's a part of their nature."

Fortunately the farmer was close enough to town that he was able to get to the doctor and get some medicine before the snake's poison went to work on him. After that though the farmer knew. If it's in the nature of a thing to hurt you, it'll do just that, no matter how kind you are to it.

# The Knee-High Man

Once upon a time there was a knee-high man. He was no taller than a person's knees. Because he was so short, he was very unhappy. He wanted to be big like everybody else.

One day he decided to ask the biggest animal he could find how he could get big. So he went to see Mr. Horse. "Mr. Horse, how can I get big like you?"

Mr. Horse said, "Well, eat a whole lot of corn. Then run around a lot. After a while you'll be as big as me."

The knee-high man did just that. He ate so much corn that his stomach hurt. Then he ran and ran and ran until his legs hurt. But he didn't get any bigger. So he decided that Mr. Horse had told him something wrong. He decided to go ask Mr. Bull.

"Mr. Bull? How can I get big like you?"

Mr. Bull said, "Eat a whole lot of grass. Then bellow and bellow as loud as you can. The first thing you know, you'll be as big as me."

So the knee-high man ate a whole field of grass. That made his stomach hurt. He bellowed and bellowed and bellowed all day and all night. That made his throat hurt. But he didn't get any bigger. So he decided that Mr. Bull was all wrong too.

Now he didn't know anyone else to ask. One night he heard Mr. Hoot Owl hooting, and he remembered that Mr. Owl knew everything. "Mr. Owl? How can I get big like Mr. Horse and Mr. Bull?"

"What do you want to be big for?" Mr. Hoot Owl asked.

"I want to be big so that when I get into a fight, I can whip everybody," the knee-high man said.

Mr. Hoot Owl hooted. "Anybody ever try to pick a fight with you?"

The knee-high man thought a minute. "Well, now that you mention it, nobody ever did try to start a fight with me."

Mr. Owl said, "Well, you don't have any reason to fight. Therefore, you don't have any reason to be bigger than you are."

"But, Mr. Owl," the knee-high man said, "I want to be big so I can see far into the distance."

Mr. Hoot Owl hooted. "If you climb a tall tree, you can see into the distance from the top."

The knee-high man was quiet for a minute. "Well, I hadn't thought of that."

Mr. Hoot Owl hooted again. "And that's what's wrong, Mr. Knee-High Man. You hadn't done any thinking at all. I'm smaller than you, and you don't see me worrying about being big. Mr. Knee-High Man, you wanted something that you didn't need."

# A Note About the Stories

My father is a Methodist minister. One characteristic of black ministers is a gift for telling stories. As a child I loved it when my father got together with other ministers on a summer evening, because I knew that I would be treated to stories for as long as I was allowed to stay up, which was never long enough. All of the stories dealt in some way or other with the black-white problem, and in the stories (but not in life), blacks got the best of whites.

As I got older, I began to learn stories from my own contemporaries on the street corner, and on trips my father and I would exchange tales for hundreds of miles. We knew we had a good one when Mother laughed, because she is not enamored of story-telling.

My senior year in college I began to study the stories and songs of my people seriously: the historical background, the layers of meaning, symbolism, etc. And in that study I became aware of a great body of animal stories. These stories came from slavery times and many of them were actually about the relations between the slave and his owner. Other stories were simply didactic, passing on to the children, in the guise of animal stories, the values of the community. And other stories were simply fun.

Today the stories which dealt with the relations of slave and master no longer have that particular level of meaning. Nonetheless, like all good stories from any folk tradition, these stories are still good ones, though their origins are now of importance only to scholars. (See the stories dealing with Mr. Rabbit, in particular, which come from the slave experience.)

So this book is simply a collection of six stories—some funny, some sad, and some didactic. Please do not feel that they cannot be changed. After all, stories are in books simply because the storyteller cannot tell his tales in person to everyone who might want to hear them. The stories I tell here can be found in other versions. "Why the Waves Have Whitecaps" and "Why Dogs Hate Cats" is in Zora Neale Hurston's *Mules and Men*. "Mr. Rabbit and Mr. Bear," "The Farmer and the Snake," and "What is Trouble?" are in Richard Dorson's *American Negro Folktales*. And "The Knee-High Man" can be found in the Langston Hughes and Arna Bontemps anthology, *The Book of Negro Folklore*.

So this is not a book as much as it is a nice way for me to tell you some of the stories I love from the heritage of my people. And if your children are anything like mine, you'll find at least two new additions to your family—Mr. Rabbit and Mr. Bear—whose adventures, I'm learning, are endless.

Julius Lester
January, 1972

# About the Author and Artist

Julius Lester is the author of books for children and young adults including *To Be a Slave,* a Newbery Medal Honor Book and winner of the Lewis Carroll Shelf Award and the Nancy Bloch Award; *Long Journey Home: Stories from Black History,* a National Book Award Finalist and a *School Library Journal* Best Book of the Year; *Who I Am; Two Love Stories,* a runnerup for the Coretta Scott King Award; and *This Strange New Feeling.* The father of four children, Mr. Lester teaches at the University of Massachusetts and lives in Amherst.

Ralph Pinto has illustrated several children's books, including *Two Wise Children* and *The Cricket Winter.* His illustrations for a paperback edition of *The Wind in the Willows* won the Award of Distinctive Merit of the Society of Illustrators.

Mr. Pinto has also worked as a graphic designer in advertising and textbooks and his paintings have been exhibited in galleries, but he derives the most enjoyment from book illustration. He and his wife and two children live in Massapequa Park, New York.